RETURN TO THE
LIBRARY OF DOOM

GHOST WRITER

BY MICHAEL DAHL

Illustrated by
Bradford Kendall

STONE ARCH BOOKS
a capstone imprint

ZONE BOOKS ARE PUBLISHED BY
STONE ARCH BOOKS
A CAPSTONE IMPRINT
151 GOOD COUNSEL DRIVE, P.O. BOX 669
MANKATO, MINNESOTA 56002
WWW.CAPSTONEPUB.COM

PRINTED IN THE UNITED STATES OF AMERICA IN NORTH MANKATO,
MINNESOTA.
032011
006110CGF11

LIBRARY OF CONGRESS CATALOGING-IN-PUBLICATION DATA
IS AVAILABLE ON THE LIBRARY OF CONGRESS WEBSITE.

ISBN: 978-1-4342-3230-4

SUMMARY: A VENGEFUL WRITER SENDS HIS ENEMIES MYSTERIOUS
BLANK BOOKS, WHICH TURN THEM INTO PHANTOMS! THE LIBRARIAN
AND THE SPECIALIST MUST SAVE A YOUNG BOY FROM THE EVIL
GHOST WRITER.

ART DIRECTOR: KAY FRASER
GRAPHIC DESIGNER: HILARY WACHOLZ
PRODUCTION SPECIALIST: MICHELLE BIEDSCHEID

COVER PHOTO CREDIT: SHUTTERSTOCK/VLADM

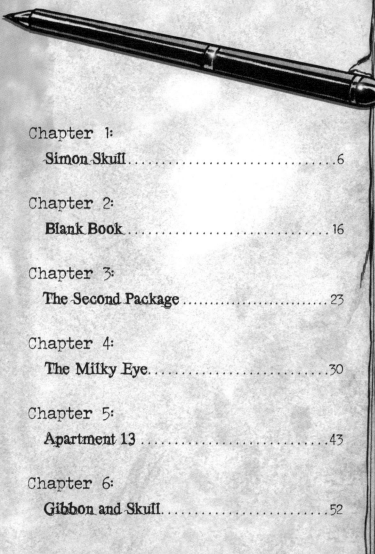

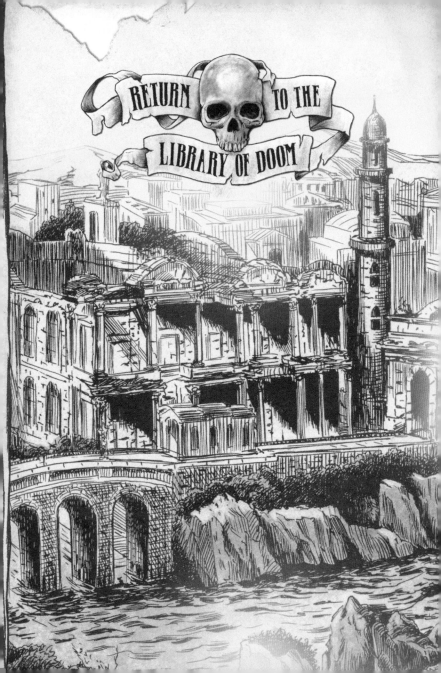

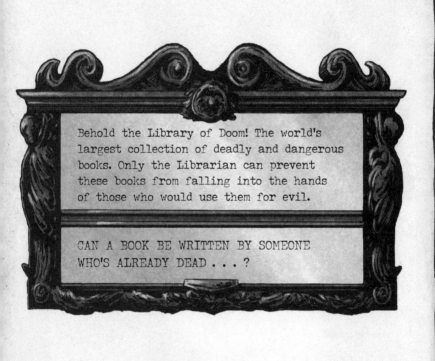

Behold the Library of Doom! The world's largest collection of deadly and dangerous books. Only the Librarian can prevent these books from falling into the hands of those who would use them for evil.

CAN A BOOK BE WRITTEN BY SOMEONE WHO'S ALREADY DEAD . . . ?

Josh steps into the bookstore and out of the pouring RAIN. He rushes up to the counter.

"Do you have any more books by Simon Skull?" Josh asks.

The young man behind the counter sneers. "Skull?" he says. "Why would you want to read that **garbage**?"

"It's been years since Simon Skull wrote a new book," the man adds. "He's **disappeared** off the face of the earth."

"I know," says Josh, **NODDING** sadly.

"His last book was *Seven Cold Fingers*.

"But I was hoping there were more. Maybe there were some books I didn't know about."

"Don't waste your time reading his books," says the man. "There are a lot of better writers out there. Besides, his books will **ROT** your brain. He only wrote about ghosts and zombies . . ."

" . . . and nameless creatures and **ALIEN** monsters," Josh adds. "I know! Isn't it great? Are you sure there aren't any more?"

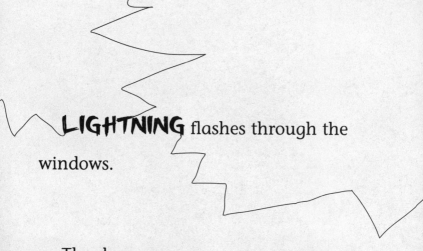

LIGHTNING flashes through the windows.

The door opens.

A woman stands in the doorway.

She has long **dark** hair. She wears a long coat over her clothes.

"Excuse me," says the woman. "Do you sell BLANK books?"

The bookseller looks DOWN at the counter.

"No. Sorry," he says. "No blank books."

The woman stares **hard** at the bookseller.

"Are there other bookstores on this street?" she asks. "They must be WARNED."

"Warned?" asks the bookseller.

"There's one on the corner," says Josh.

Lightning flashes again and the woman is gone.

Chapter 2

Blank Book

Josh RUSHES out into the storm.

He races to the bookstore on the corner.

What did that woman mean? he wonders.

Josh **steps** inside the second store
and brushes the rain from his sleeves.

The bookstore is **SILENT**. The
woman is not here.

"Hello?" calls Josh. No one answers.

There is no one behind the counter.

Maybe the owner is helping another customer, Josh thinks.

The bookstore is crammed full of TALL shelves and shadowy passages.

A dim lamp burns on the old counter.

Josh notices a package on the counter. The wrapping paper is **torn** open. A book lies inside.

He sees a small title stamped in GOLD on the cover.

The book **RISES** a few inches into the air.

It falls back down onto the counter with a thump.

Josh steps back. Then he hears a soft SCRATCHING sound.

"Who's there?" croaks Josh. His throat is dry.

The scratching, crinkling sound GR**O**W**S** louder.

The brown wrapping paper on the counter is moving.

It slowly crunches itself into a ball.

Josh stares in HORROR.

Then the paper unfolds itself and lies **FLAT** on the counter.

On the paper, Josh sees **words** that weren't there before.

Chapter 3

The Second Package

Josh races back to the other bookstore. He bursts through the door.

"HELP!" he shouts.

But the young man behind the counter is gone.

Josh's skin begins to **tingle**.

On the counter he sees a package.
Its wrapping paper is **torn** open too.

"Is anyone here?" shouts Josh.

The bookstore is **SOUNDLESS**.

Nothing moves. The paper lies still.

Josh moves slowly toward the counter.

He wants to see if there is a book
inside this wrapping paper, too.

Josh steps behind the counter for a
closer look.

His shoe hits a book. Josh bends down
and picks it up.

It is a blank book.

Another one, Josh tells himself.

He places the book on the counter.

Then he carefully pokes the torn wrapping paper.

It doesn't move.

Josh *leans* closer to the paper.

A return address is **WRITTEN** on
one of the corners.

"Simon Skull!" shouts Josh.

Skull's address is written underneath his name.

"I don't believe it," Josh whispers.

Suddenly, the blank book floats above the counter. Then it **hurls** itself through the store's window.

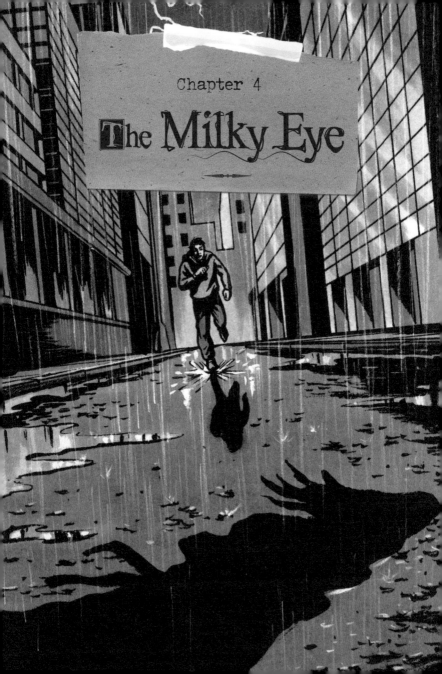

Chapter 4

The Milky Eye

Lightning **crackles** above the city streets.

As Josh runs toward King Street, he sees a shadow up ahead.

The dark shape reminds him of the **STRANGE** woman back at the bookstore.

She was looking for blank books, thinks Josh.

Several minutes later, Josh finds the address.

It is an old, **CRUMBLING** building.

A doorman in a faded uniform stands outside.

The man is all skin and **BONES**.

He smiles at Josh.

As Josh nears the building, the doorman leans toward him. He has one **green** eye and one that's **white** as milk.

The doorman stares at Josh.

He opens the **HEAVY** door and Josh steps inside.

A list of names covers the wall of the narrow entrance.

Beside each name is the apartment number.

Josh runs his finger down the list.

"There's no **SKULL** anywhere," he says.

Then he looks for Apartment **13**.

Next to the number is the name:

HARRY GIBBON

Josh **frowns**.

Could that be his real name? Josh wonders. *Maybe he uses a* fake *name so people won't bother him.*

Josh puts his hands in his jacket pockets. *I wonder if he'll think I'm bothering him.*

But I'm his **biggest** fan, thinks Josh.
I just want to tell him how great he is.
How he needs to write another book.

That wouldn't be bothering him,
would it? Josh is not sure.

The outside door opens with a
LOUD sucking sound. The doorman
sticks his head inside.

"You know where you're going?" he asks Josh.

His milky eye **gleams** in the dim light.

"Sure, sure," says Josh. "I just wanted to **dry** off before I went upstairs."

The doorman slowly nods his head. Josh steps into the huge, **DARK** lobby.

41

His **wet** shoes squeak against the smooth marble floor.

"Are you sure you know where you're going?" repeats the doorman.

"I'm going upstairs now," says Josh.

He puts his hand on the cool stone railing and CLIMBS the steps.

Chapter 5

Apartment 13

Josh hears something scratching in the hallways.

?

Rats?

?

The sound reminds him of the wrapping paper that **crunched** itself into a ball.

The sound GROWS louder as Josh nears a door at the end of a hallway.

It is Apartment 13.

The door is partly open.

Josh hears the SCRATCHING sound. It's coming from inside the apartment.

He also hears a woman's voice.

"Scribble, scribble, scribble, Mr.
Gibbon?"

Josh recognizes the voice.

As he steps into the apartment, he
sees the **strange** woman from the
bookstore.

She is speaking to a man sitting at a
desk. His face and hands are hidden in
shadow.

The man holds a pen in his right
hand. He is **WRITING** in a blank book.

A stack of blank books sits next to
him on the <u>FLOOR</u>.

"You must **stop** this," says the woman.

The man looks up at her.

"I thought you liked books," he says.
"You like lots and lots of BOOKS. Here.
Have this one!"

He **throws** a book into her hands. As soon as her fingers touch the blank book, the woman begins to FADE.

HA! HA!

The man laughs. HA!

HA!

"All those people who hated my Simon Skull books — they said I was nothing! Said I was just a blank!" shouts the man. "Well, now they're all blank! Everyone who touches these books turns into a big, **fat** nothing. A zero! A ghost!"

Josh stares in horror.

The blank book **hovers** above

the floor.

The woman must still be holding it, he

thinks. *She's still there, but she's not there.*

A ghost.

Chapter 6

Gibbon and Skull

Josh feels the **HAIR** on the back of his neck standing up.

The shadowy man **turns** and stares.

"You!" cries the man. "Who are you?"

Josh's throat feels **DRY**.

"Uh . . . uh . . ." he croaks. "I'm just a fan . . ."

A hand **grips** his shoulder.

Josh looks up and sees a man standing behind him.

The man is TALL. He wears a long black coat and dark glasses.

The man looks down at Josh and smiles. "I think," he says, "that **Mr. Gibbon** was talking to me."

The shadowy writer JUMPS up from
his chair.

"You're the Librarian," he says.

The **DARK** stranger nods.

"And you have my blank books," the Librarian says. "And my friend."

The Librarian raises his arm and points to the blank book, still floating in midair. It flies into his hand.

The Librarian pulls a pen from his pocket. He crosses out the word that the Skull had written.

Then he writes another word: **SPECIALIST**.

The woman reappears in the middle of the apartment.

She looks at the Librarian. "Thanks," she says.

Josh notices something. The shadowy author has **VANISHED**. "Simon Skull!" cries Josh. "He's gone!"

Josh looks up at the two **strangers**. "You have to find him. You have to stop him!"

The Librarian looks grim. "Don't worry. That was only his shadow," he says.

He nods toward another door in the
apartment. Josh peeks into the room.

A body is lying on a **dirty** bed.

"It's Skull," says the Specialist. "Or
Gibbon. Whatever his real name is.
And he's been there for quite some
time."

Slowly, Josh ENTERS the room.

He sees the man's head **lying** on the pillow.

The man does not move. The man does not breathe.

His eyes stare at the ceiling. One **green** eye and one as white as milk.

AUTHOR

Michael Dahl is the author of more than 200 books for children and young adults. He has won the AEP Distinguished Achievement Award three times for his nonfiction. His Finnegan Zwake mystery series was shortlisted twice by the Anthony and Agatha awards. He has also written the Dragonblood series. He is a featured speaker at conferences around the country on graphic novels and high-interest books for boys.

ILLUSTRATOR

Bradford Kendall has enjoyed drawing for as long as he can remember. As a boy, he loved to read comic books and watch old monster movies. He graduated from Rhode Island School of Design with a BFA in Illustration. He has owned his own commercial art business since 1983, and lives in Providence, Rhode Island, with his wife, Leigh, and their two children Lily and Stephen. They also have a cat named Hansel and a dog named Gretel.

GLOSSARY

alien (AY-lee-uhn)—a creature from another planet

creatures (KREE-churz)—living beings

disappeared (diss-uh-PIHRD)—went out of sight

doorman (DOR-man)—a person who works at an apartment building and lets people in or out

grim (GRIM)—gloomy, stern, or unpleasant

horror (HOR-ur)—great fear, terror, or shock

nameless (NAYM-less)—having no name

recognizes (REK-uhg-nize-iz)—sees or hears someone and knows who the person is

return address (ri-TURN AD-ress)—the address of the person who sent a letter or package, written so that the mail can be returned to them if necessary

sneers (SNIHRZ)—smiles in a hateful, mocking way

warned (WORND)—told a person about a danger or something that might happen

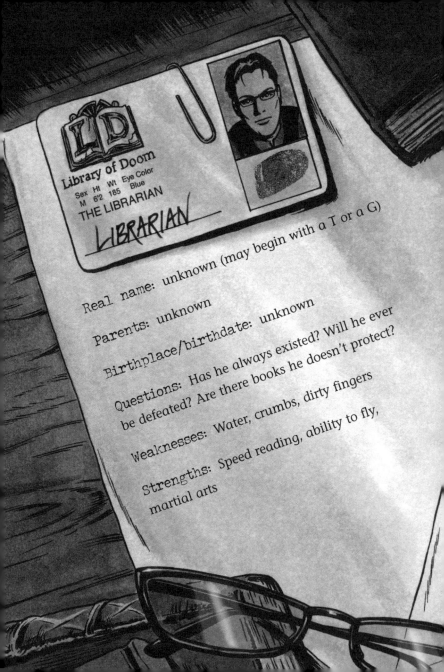

Library of Doom

Sex | Ht | Wt | Eye Color
M | 6'2 | 185 | Blue

THE LIBRARIAN

LIBRARIAN

Real name: unknown (may begin with a T or a G)

Parents: unknown

Birthplace/birthdate: unknown

Questions: Has he always existed? Will he ever be defeated? Are there books he doesn't protect?

Weaknesses: Water, crumbs, dirty fingers

Strengths: Speed reading, ability to fly, martial arts

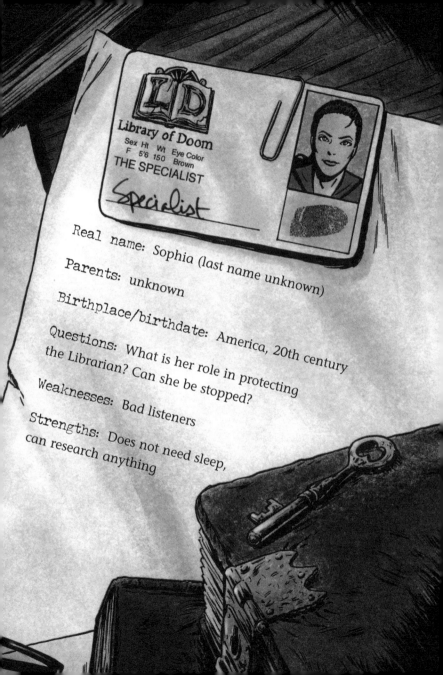

After the Librarian defeated it, Harry Gibbon's shadow retreated to wherever shadows go. But the legend of Gibbon himself lives on.

Though his books, written under the pen name Simon Skull, were all bestsellers, many critics said that he could tell a great story, but that he wasn't a good writer. Gibbon, who had received a PhD. in English, hated hearing those comments. He became stranger and stranger, eventually refusing to leave his tiny apartment for months at a time.

Eventually, it seems, Harry Gibbon got his revenge. But the Librarian — who prefers a good story to perfect grammar any time — had to defeat Harry Gibbon's shadow, for fear he'd make more books blank.

DISCUSSION QUESTIONS

1. What happened to Harry Gibbon/Simon Skull?

2. Do you know the difference between a good story and a well-written story? Which do you prefer to read? Talk about it.

3. Josh wants to tell **SIMON SKULL** that Skull is his favorite author. But he worries that it would be bothering Mr. Skull. What do you think? Is it impolite to tell a well-known person your opinion of his or her work?

WRITING PROMPTS

1. Make your own BLANK BOOK using paper and a stapler. Fill it with whatever you want!

2. Try writing this story from Harry Gibbon/Simon Skull's point of view. What does he think? What does he see? How does he feel?

3. Who's your FAVORITE author? Write a letter to that person.